KT-508-992

HORRID HENRY'S
Monster Movie

Francesca Simon spent her childhood on the beach
in California, and then went to Yale and Oxford
Universities to study Medieval History and Literature.
She now lives in London with her family. She has
written more than 50 books and won the Children's
Book of the Year in 2008 at the Galaxy British Book
Awards for *Horrid Henry and the Abominable Snowman*.

Also by Francesca Simon

Don't Cook Cinderella
Helping Hercules

and for younger readers

Café at the Edge of the Moon
Mr P's Naughty Book
The Parent Swap Shop
Spider School
The Topsy-Turvies
Runaway Duckling
Meet the Gang

There is a complete list of **Horrid Henry**
titles at the end of the book.

Visit Horrid Henry's website at
www.horridhenry.co.uk for competitions,
games, downloads and a monthly newsletter

HORRID HENRY'S
Monster Movie

Francesca Simon
Illustrated by Tony Ross

Orion
Children's Books

ORION CHILDREN'S BOOKS

First published in Great Britain in 2012 by Orion Children's Books
This edition published in 2016 by Hodder and Stoughton

22

Text copyright © Francesca Simon, 2012
Illustrations copyright © Tony Ross, 2012

The moral rights of the author and illustrator have been asserted.

*All characters and events in this publication, other than those clearly
in the public domain, are fictitious and any resemblance to
real persons, living or dead, is purely coincidental.*

All rights reserved.
No part of this publication may be reproduced, stored in
a retrieval system, or transmitted, in any form or by any means, without
the prior permission in writing of the publisher, nor be otherwise circulated
in any form of binding or cover other than that in which it is published
and without a similar condition including this condition being
imposed on the subsequent purchaser.

A CIP catalogue record for this book
is available from the British Library.

ISBN 978 1 4072 4849 3

Printed and bound in Great Britain by Clays Ltd, Elcograf S.p.A.

The paper and board used in this book are
made from wood from responsible sources.

Orion Children's Books
An imprint of
Hachette Children's Group
Part of Hodder and Stoughton
Carmelite House
50 Victoria Embankment
London EC4Y 0DZ

An Hachette UK Company
www.hachette.co.uk

www.hachettechildrens.co.uk
www.horridhenry.co.uk

For Emily Lethbridge

CONTENTS

1

....

HORRiD HENRY'S MONSTER MOVIE

Horrid Henry loved scary movies. He loved nothing more than curling up on the comfy black chair with a huge bag of popcorn and a Fizzywizz drink, and jumping out of his seat in shock every few minutes. He loved wailing ghosts, oozing swamps, and bloodthirsty monsters. No film was too scary or too creepy for Horrid Henry. MWAHAHAHAHAHAHA!

Perfect Peter hated scary movies. He hated nothing more than hiding behind the comfy black chair covering his eyes and jumping out of his skin in shock every few seconds. He hated ghosts and swamps and monsters. Even Santa Claus saying 'ho ho ho' too loudly scared him.

Thanks to Peter being the biggest scaredy-cat who ever lived, Mum and Dad would never take Henry to see any scary films.

And now, the scariest, most frightening, most terrible film ever was in town. Horrid Henry was desperate to see it.

'You're not seeing that film and that's final,' said Mum.

'Absolutely no way,' said Dad. 'Far too scary.'

'But I love scary movies!' shrieked Horrid Henry.

'I don't,' said Mum.

'I don't,' said Dad.

'I hate scary movies,' said Perfect Peter.
'Please can we see *The Big Bunny Caper*
instead?'

'NO!' shrieked Horrid Henry.

'Stop shouting, Henry,' said Mum.

'But everyone's seen *The Vampire
Zombie Werewolf*,' moaned Horrid Henry.
'Everyone but me.'

Moody Margaret had seen it, and said
it was the best horror film ever.

Fiery Fiona had seen it three times.
'And I'm seeing it three more times,' she
squealed.

Rude Ralph said he'd run screaming from the cinema.

AAAARRRRGGGGHHHHHH.

Horrid Henry thought he would explode he wanted to see *The Vampire Zombie Werewolf* so much. But no. The film came and went, and Horrid Henry wailed and gnashed.

So he couldn't believe his luck when Rude Ralph came up to him one day at playtime and said:

'I've got *The Vampire Zombie*

Werewolf film on DVD. Want to come over and watch it after school?'

Did he ever!

Horrid Henry squeezed onto the sofa between Rude Ralph and Brainy Brian. Dizzy Dave sat on the floor next to Jolly Josh and Aerobic Al. Anxious Andrew sat on a chair. He'd already covered his face with his hands. Even Moody Margaret and Sour Susan were there, squabbling over who got to sit in the armchair and who had to sit on the floor.

'OK everyone, this is it,' said Rude Ralph. 'The scariest film ever. Are we ready?'

'Yeah!'

Horrid Henry gripped the sofa as the eerie piano music started.

There was a deep, dark forest.

'I'm scared!' wailed Anxious Andrew.

'Nothing's happened yet,' said Horrid Henry.

A boy and a girl ran through the shivery, shadowy trees.

'Is it safe to look?' gasped Anxious Andrew.

'Shhh,' said Moody Margaret.

'You shhh!' said Horrid Henry.

'MWAHAAAAHAAAAHAHAHAA!' bellowed Dizzy Dave.

'I'm scared!' shrieked Anxious Andrew.

'Shut up!' shouted Rude Ralph.

The pale girl stopped running and turned to the bandaged boy.

'I can't kiss you or I'll turn into a zombie,' sulked the girl.

'I can't kiss *you* or *I'll* turn into a vampire,' scowled the boy.

'But our love is so strong!' wailed the vampire girl and the zombie boy.

'Not as strong as me!' howled the werewolf, leaping out from behind a tree stump.

'AAAAAAAARRRRGGGHHH!' screeched Anxious Andrew.

'SHUT UP!' shouted Henry and Ralph.

'Leave her alone, you walking bandage,' said the werewolf.

'Leave him alone, you smelly fur ball,' said the vampire.

'This isn't scary,' said Horrid Henry.

'Shh,' said Margaret.

'Go away!' shouted the zombie.

'You go away, you big meanie,' snarled the werewolf.

'Don't you know that two's company and three's a crowd?' hissed the vampire.

'I challenge you both to an arm-wrestling contest,' howled the werewolf. 'The winner gets to keep the arms.'

'Or in your case the paws,' sniffed the vampire.

'This is the worst film I've ever seen,' said Horrid Henry.

'Shut up, Henry,' said Margaret.

'We're trying to watch,' said Susan.

'Ralph, I thought you said this was a really scary film,' hissed Henry. 'Have you *actually* seen it before?'

Rude Ralph looked at the floor.

'No,' admitted Ralph. 'But everyone said they'd seen it and I didn't want to be left out.'

'Margaret's a big fat liar too,' said Susan. 'She never saw it either.'

'Shut up, Susan!' shrieked Margaret.

'Awhoooooooo,' howled the werewolf.

Horrid Henry was disgusted. He could make a *much* scarier film. In fact . . . what was stopping him? Who better to make the scariest film of all time than

Henry? How hard could it be to make
a film? You just pointed a camera and
yelled, 'Action!' Then he'd be rich rich
rich. He'd need a spare house just to
stash all his cash. And he'd be famous,
too. Everyone would be begging
for a role in one of his mega-horror
blockbusters. *Please can we be in your new
monster film?* Mum and Dad and Peter
would beg. Well, they could beg as
long as they liked. He'd give them his
autograph, but that would be *it*.

Henry could see the poster now:

HENRY PRODUCTIONS PRESENT:

THE UNDEAD DEMON MONSTER WHO WOULD NOT DIE

Starring HENRY as The Monster

Written and Filmed and Directed by
HENRY

'I could make a *really* scary film,' said Henry.

'Not as scary as the film *I* could make,' said Margaret.

'Ha!' said Henry. 'Your scary film wouldn't scare a toddler.'

'Ha!' said Margaret. *'Your* scary film would make a baby laugh.'

'Oh yeah?' said Henry.

'Yeah,' said Margaret.

'Well, we'll just see about that,' said Henry.

Horrid Henry walked around his garden, clutching Mum's camcorder. He could turn the garden into a swamp . . . flood a few flower beds . . . rip up the lawn and throw buckets of mud at the windows as the monster squelched his monstrous way through the undergrowth, growling and devouring, biting and—

'Henry, can I be in your movie?' said Peter.

'No,' said Henry. 'I'm making a scary

monster film. No nappy babies.'

'I am not a nappy baby,' said Peter.

'Are too.'

'Am not. Mum! Henry won't let me be in his film.'

'Henry!' yelled Mum. 'Let Peter be in your film or you can't borrow the camcorder.'

Gah! Why did everyone always get in his way? How could Henry be a

great director if other people told him
who to put in his film?

'Okay Peter,' said Henry, scowling.
'You can be Best Boy.'

Best Boy! That sounded super. Wow.
That was a lot better than Peter had
hoped.

'Best Boy!' shouted Horrid Henry.
'Get the snack table ready.'

'*Snack* table?' said Peter.

'Setting up the snack table is the most
important part of making a movie,' said
Henry. 'So I want biscuits and crisps and

Fizzywizz drinks – NOW!' he bellowed.
'It's hungry work making a film.'

Film-making next door at Moody
Margaret's house was also proceeding
slowly.

'How come I have to move the
furniture?' said Susan. 'You said I could
be in your movie.'

'Because *I'm* the director,' said
Margaret. 'So *I* decide.'

'Margaret, you can be the monster
in *my* film. No need for any make–up,'
shouted Horrid Henry over the wall.

'Shut up, Henry,' said Margaret.
'Susan. Start walking down the path.'

'BOOOOOOOOOOOOO,'
shouted Horrid Henry.
'BOOOOOOOOOOOOO.'

'Cut!' yelled Margaret. 'Quiet!' she
screamed. 'I'm making a movie here.'

★

'Peter, hold the torch and shine the spotlight on me,' ordered Henry.

'Hold the torch?' said Peter.

'It's very important,' said Henry.

'Mum said you had to let me *be* in your movie,' said Peter. 'Or I'm telling on you.'

Horrid Henry glared at Perfect Peter.

Perfect Peter glared at Horrid Henry.

'Mum!' screamed Peter.

'Okay, you can be in the movie,' said Henry.

'Stop being horrid, Henry,' shouted Mum. 'Or you hand back that camera instantly.'

'I'm not being horrid; that's in the movie,' lied Henry.

Perfect Peter opened his mouth and then closed it.

'So what's my part?' said Peter.

16

★

Perfect Peter stood on the bench in the
front garden.

'Now say your line, "I am too horrible
to live," and jump off the bench into
the crocodile-filled moat, where you are
eaten alive and drown,' said Henry.

'I don't want to say that,' said Peter.

Horrid Henry lowered the camera.
'Do you want to be in the film or don't
you?' he hissed.

17

'I am too horrible to live,' muttered
Peter.

'Louder!' said Henry.

'I am too horrible to live,' said Peter,
a fraction louder.

'And as you drown, scream out, "and I
have smelly pants",' said Henry.

'*What*?' said Peter.

Tee hee, thought Horrid Henry.

'But how come you get to play all
the other parts, *and* dance, *and* sing,
and all I get to do is walk about going

18

wooooooo?' said Susan sourly in next door's garden.

'Because it's *my* movie,' said Margaret.

'Keep it down, we're filming here,' said Henry. 'Now Peter, you are walking down the garden path out into the street—'

'I thought I'd just drowned,' said Peter.

Henry rolled his eyes.

'No dummy, this is a horror film. You *rose* from the dead, and now you're walking down the path singing this song, just before the hairy scary monster leaps out of the bushes and rips you to shreds.

'Wibble bibble dribble pants
Bibble baby wibble pants
Wibble pants wibble pants
Dribble dribble dribble pants,'

sang Horrid Henry.

Perfect Peter hesitated. 'But Henry, why would my character sing that song?'

Henry glared at Peter.

'Because I'm the director and I say so,' said Henry.

Perfect Peter's lip trembled. He started walking.

'Wibble bibble dribble pants
Bibble baby wibble pants
Wibble pants wib–'

'I don't want to!' came a screech from next door's front garden.

'Susan, you *have* to be covered up in a sheet,' said Margaret.

'But no one will see my face and know it's me,' said Susan.

'Duh,' said Margaret. 'You're playing a ghost.'

Sour Susan flung off the sheet.

'Well I quit,' said Susan.

'You're fired!' shouted Margaret.

'I don't want to sing that dribble pants song,' said Peter.

'Then you're fired!' screamed Henry.

'No!' screamed Perfect Peter. 'I quit.' And he ran out of the front garden gate, shrieking and wailing.

Wow, thought Horrid Henry. He chased after Peter, filming.

'I've had it!' screamed Sour Susan. 'I don't want to be in your stupid film!'

She ran off down the road, shrieking and wailing.

Margaret chased after her, filming.

Cool, thought Horrid Henry, what a perfect end for his film, the puny wimp running off terrified—

BUMP!

Susan and Peter collided and sprawled flat on the pavement.

CRASH!

Henry and Margaret tripped over the screaming Peter and Susan.

SMASH!

Horrid Henry dropped his camcorder.

SMASH!

Moody Margaret dropped *her* camcorder.

OOPS.

Horrid Henry stared down at the twisted broken metal as his monster movie lay shattered on the concrete path.

WHOOPS.

Moody Margaret stared down at the cracked camcorder as her Hollywood horror film lay in pieces on the ground.

'Henry!' hissed Margaret.

'Margaret!' hissed Henry.

'This is all your fault!' they wailed.

2

HORRID HENRY'S HORRID WEEKEND

'NOOOOOOOOO!' screamed Horrid
Henry. 'I don't want to spend the
weekend with Steve.'

'Don't be horrid, Henry,' said Mum.
'It's very kind of Aunt Ruby to invite us
down for the weekend.'

'But I hate Aunt Ruby!' shrieked
Henry. 'And I hate Steve and I hate you!'

'I can't wait to go,' said Perfect Peter.

'Shut up, Peter!' howled Henry.

'Don't tell your brother to shut up,'
shouted Mum.

'Shut up! Shut up! Shut up!' And
Horrid Henry fell to the floor wailing
and screaming and kicking.

Stuck-Up Steve was Horrid Henry's
hideous cousin. Steve hated Henry.
Henry hated him. The last time Henry
had seen Steve, Henry had tricked
him into thinking there was a monster
under his bed. Steve had sworn revenge.
Then there was the other time at the
restaurant when . . . well, Horrid Henry
thought it would be a good idea to
avoid Steve until his cousin was grown-
up and in prison for crimes against
humanity.

And now his mean, horrible parents were forcing him to spend a whole precious weekend with the toadiest, wormiest, smelliest boy who ever slimed out of a swamp.

Mum sighed. 'We're going and that's that. Ruby says Steve is having a lovely friend over so that should be extra fun.'

Henry stopped screaming and kicking. Maybe Steve's friend wouldn't be a stuck-up monster. Maybe *he'd* been forced to waste his weekend with Steve, too. After all, who'd volunteer to spend time with Steve? Maybe together they could squish Stuck-Up Steve once and for all.

Ding dong.

Horrid Henry, Perfect Peter, Mum and Dad stood outside Rich Aunt Ruby's enormous house on a grey, drizzly day. Steve opened the massive front door.

'Oh,' he sneered. 'It's you.'

Steve opened the present Mum had brought. It was a small flashlight. Steve put it down.

'I already have a much better one,' he said.

'Oh,' said Mum.

Another boy stood beside him. A boy who looked vaguely familiar. A boy . . . Horrid Henry gasped. Oh no. It was Bill. Bossy Bill. The horrible son of Dad's boss. Henry had once tricked Bill into photocopying his bottom. Bill had sworn revenge. Horrid Henry's insides turned to jelly. Trust Stuck-Up Steve to be friends with Bossy Bill. It was bad enough being trapped in a house with one Arch-Enemy. Now he was stuck in a house with TWO . . .

Stuck-up Steve scowled at Henry.
'You're wearing that old shirt of mine,'
he said. 'Don't your parents ever buy
you new clothes?'

Bossy Bill snorted.

'Steve,' said Aunt Ruby. 'Don't be
rude.'

'I wasn't,' said Steve. 'I was just asking.
No harm in asking, is there?'

'No,' said Horrid Henry. He smiled
at Steve. 'So when will Aunt Ruby buy
you a new face?'

'Henry,' said Mum. 'Don't be rude.'

'I was just asking,' said Henry. 'No harm in asking, is there?' he added, glaring at Steve.

Steve glared back.

Aunt Ruby beamed. 'Henry, Steve and Bill are taking you to their friend Tim's paintballing party.'

'Won't that be fun,' said Mum.

Peter looked frightened.

'Don't worry, Peter,' said Aunt Ruby, 'you can help me plant seedlings while the older boys are out.'

Peter beamed. 'Thank you,' he said. 'I don't like paintballing. Too messy and scary.'

Paintballing! Horrid Henry loved paintballing. The chance to splat Steve and Bill with ooey gooey globs of paint . . . hmmm, maybe the weekend was looking up.

'Great!' said Horrid Henry.

'How nice,' said Rich Aunt Ruby,
'you boys already know each other.
Think how much fun you're all going to
have sharing Steve's bedroom together.'

Uh-oh, thought Horrid Henry.

'Yeah!' said Stuck-Up Steve. 'We're
looking forward to sharing a room with
Henry.' His piggy eyes gleamed.

'Yeah!' said Bossy Bill. 'I can't wait.'
His piggy eyes gleamed.

31

'Yeah,' said Horrid Henry. He wouldn't be sleeping a wink.

Horrid Henry looked around the enormous high-ceilinged bedroom he'd be sharing with his two evil enemies for two very long days and one very long night. There was a bunk-bed, which Steve and Bill had already nabbed, and two single beds. Steve's bedroom shelves were stuffed with zillions of new toys and games, as usual.

Bill and Steve smirked at each other. Henry scowled at them. What were they plotting?

'Don't you dare touch my Super-Blooper Blaster,' said Steve.

'Don't you dare touch my Demon Dagger Sabre,' said Bill.

A Super-Blooper Blaster! A Demon Dagger Sabre! Trust Bill and Steve to

have the two best toys in the world . . .
Rats.

'Don't worry,' said Henry. 'I don't
play with baby toys.'

'Oh yeah,' said Stuck-Up Steve. 'Bet
you're too much of a baby to jump off
my top bunk onto your bed.'

'Am not,' said Henry.

'We're not allowed to jump on beds,'
said Perfect Peter.

'We're not allowed,' mimicked Steve.
'I thought you were too poor to even
have beds.'

'Ha ha,' said Henry.

'Chicken. Chicken. Scaredy cat,'
sneered Bossy Bill.

'Squawk!' said Stuck-Up Steve. 'I
knew you'd be too scared, chicken.'

That did it. *No* one called Horrid
Henry chicken and lived. As if he,
Henry, leader of a pirate gang, would be

afraid to jump off a top bunk. Ha.

'Don't do it, Henry,' said Perfect Peter.

'Shut up, worm,' said Henry.

'But it's so high,' squealed Peter, squeezing his eyes shut.

Horrid Henry clambered up the ladder and stepped onto the top bunk. 'It's nothing,' he lied. 'I've jumped off MUCH higher.'

'Well, go on then,' said Stuck-Up Steve.

Boing! Horrid Henry bounced.

Boing! Horrid Henry bounced higher. Whee! This bed was very springy.

'We're waiting, chicken,' said Bossy Bill.

BOING! BOING! Horrid Henry bent his knees, then – – – leap! He jumped onto the single bed below.

SMASH!
Horrid Henry crashed to the floor as the bed collapsed beneath him.

Huh? What? How could he have broken the bed? He hadn't heard any breaking sounds.

It was as if . . . as if . . .

Mum, Dad and Aunt Ruby ran into the room.

'Henry broke the bed,' said Stuck-Up Steve.

'We tried to stop him,' said Bossy Bill, 'but Henry insisted on jumping.'

'But . . . but . . .' said Horrid Henry.

'Henry!' wailed Mum. 'You horrid boy.'

'How could you be so horrid?' said Dad. 'No pocket money for a year. Ruby, I'm so sorry.'

Aunt Ruby pursed her lips. 'These things happen,' she said.

'And no paintballing party for you,' said Mum.

What?

'No!' wailed Henry.

Then Horrid Henry saw a horrible
sight. Behind Aunt Ruby's back, Steve
and Bill were covering their mouths
and laughing. Henry realised the terrible
truth. Bill and Steve had tricked him.

They'd broken the bed. And now *he'd*
got the blame.

'But I didn't break it!' screamed Henry.

'Yes you did, Henry,' said Peter. 'I
saw you.'

AAAARRRRGGGGHHHH! Horrid
Henry leapt at Peter. He was a storm

god hurling thunderbolts at a foolish mortal.

'AAAIIIEEEEEE!' squealed Perfect Peter.

'Henry! Stop it!' shrieked Mum. 'Leave your brother alone.'

Nah nah ne nah nah mouthed Steve behind Aunt Ruby's back.

'Isn't it lovely how nicely the boys are playing together?' said Aunt Ruby.

'Yes, isn't it?' said Mum.

'Not surprising,' said Aunt Ruby, beaming. 'After all, Steve is such a polite, friendly boy, I've never met anyone who didn't love him.'

Snore! Snore! Snore!

Horrid Henry lay on a mattress listening to hideous snoring sounds. He'd stayed awake for hours, just in case they tried anything horrible, like

pouring water on his head, or stuffing
frogs in his bed. Which was what he was
going to do to Peter, the moment he
got home.

Henry had just spent the most horrible
Saturday of his life. He'd begged to go to
the paintballing party. He'd pleaded to go
to the paintballing party. He'd screamed
about going to the paintballing party. But
no. His mean, horrible parents wouldn't
budge. And it was all Steve and Bill's fault.
They'd tripped him going down the stairs.

They'd kicked him under the table at dinner (and then complained that he was kicking *them*). And every time Aunt Ruby's back was turned they stuck out their tongues and jeered: 'We're going paintballing, and you're not.'

He had to get to that party. And he had to be revenged. But how? How? His two Arch-Enemies had banded together and struck the first blow. Could he booby-trap their beds and remove a few slats? Unfortunately, everyone would know *he'd* done it and he'd be in even more trouble than he was now.

Scare them? Tell them there was a monster under the bed? Hmmm. He knew Steve was as big a scaredy cat as Peter. But he'd already done that once. He didn't think Steve would fall for it again.

Get them into trouble? Turn them against each other? Steal their best toys and hide them? Hmmm. Hmmm. Horrid Henry thought and thought. He had to be revenged. He had to.

Tweet tweet. It was Sunday morning. The birds were singing. The sun was shining. The—

Yank!

Bossy Bill and Stuck-Up Steve pulled off his duvet.

'Nah na ne nah nah, we-ee beat you,' crowed Bill.

'Nah na ne nah nah, we got you into trouble,' crowed Steve.

Horrid Henry scowled. Time to put Operation Revenge into action.

'Bill thinks you're bossy, Steve,' said Henry. 'He told me.'

'Didn't,' said Bossy Bill.

'And Steve thinks you're stuck-up, Bill,' added Henry sweetly.

'No I don't,' said Steve.

'Then why'd you tell me that?' said Horrid Henry.

Steve stuck his nose in the air. 'Nice try Henry, you big loser,' said Stuck-Up Steve. 'Just ignore him, Bill.'

'Henry, it's not nice to tell lies,' said Perfect Peter.

'Shut up, worm,' snarled Horrid Henry.

Rats.

Time for plan B.

Except he didn't have a plan B.

'I can't wait for Tim's party,' said Bossy Bill. 'You never know what's going to happen.'

'Yeah, remember when he told us he was having a pirate party and instead we went to the Wild West Theme Park!' said Steve.

'Or when he said we were having a sleepover, and instead we all went to a Manic Buzzards concert.'

'And Tim gives the best party bags. Last year everyone got a Deluxe Demon Dagger Sabre,' said Steve. 'Wonder what he'll give this year? Oh, I forgot, Henry won't be coming to the party.'

'Too bad you can't come, Henry,' sneered Bossy Bill.

'Yeah, too bad,' sneered Stuck-Up Steve. 'Not.'

ARRRRGGGHH. Horrid Henry's blood boiled. He couldn't decide what was worse, listening to them crow about having got him into so much trouble, or brag about the great party they were going to and he wasn't.

'I can't wait to find out what surprises he'll have in store this year,' said Bill.

'Yeah,' said Steve.

Who cares? thought Horrid Henry.
Unless Tim was planning to throw Bill
and Steve into a shark tank. That would
be a nice surprise. Unless of course . . .

And then suddenly Horrid Henry had
a brilliant, spectacular idea. It was so
brilliant, and so spectacular, that for a
moment he wondered whether he
could stop himself from flinging open
the window and shouting his plan out
loud. Oh wow. Oh wow. It was risky.
It was dangerous. But if it worked, he
would have the best revenge ever in
the history of the world. No, the
history of the solar system. No, the
history of the universe!

It was an hour before the party. Horrid
Henry was counting the seconds until
he could escape.

Aunt Ruby popped her head round
the door waving an envelope.

'Letter for you boys,' she said.

Steve snatched it and tore it open.

Dear Steve and Bill

Party of the year update.
Everyone must come to my house
wearing pyjamas (you'll find
out why later, but don't be
surprised if we all end up in
a film – shhhh). It'll be a real
laugh. Make sure to bring
your favourite soft toys, too,
and wear your fluffiest
slippers. Hollywood, here
we come!

Tim

'He must be planning something
amazing,' said Bill.

'I bet we're all going to be acting in a

film!' said Steve.

'Yeah!' said Bill.

'Too bad *you* won't, Henry,' said Stuck-Up Steve.

'You're so lucky,' said Henry. 'I wish I were going.'

Mum looked at Dad.

Dad looked at Mum.

Henry held his breath.

'Well, you can't, Henry, and that's final,' said Mum.

'It's so unfair!' shrieked Henry.

Henry's parents dropped Steve and Bill off at Tim's party on their way home. Steve was in his blue bunny pyjamas and blue bunny fluffy slippers, and clutching a panda.

Bill was in his yellow duckling pyjamas and yellow duckling fluffy slippers, and clutching his monkey.

'Shame you can't come, Henry,' said
Steve, smirking. 'But we'll be sure to tell
you all about it.'

'Do,' said Henry, as Mum drove off.

Horrid Henry heard squeals of laughter
at Hoity-Toity Tim's front door. Bill
and Steve stood frozen. Then they
started to wave frantically at the car.

'Are they saying something?' said Mum, glancing in the rear-view mirror.

'Nah, just waving goodbye,' said Horrid Henry. He rolled down his window.

'Have fun, guys!'

3

HORRID HENRY'S GRUMP CARD

'I've been so good!' shrieked Horrid Henry. 'Why can't I have a grump card?'

'You have not been good,' said Mum.

'You've been awful,' said Dad.

'No I haven't,' said Henry.

Mum sighed. 'Just today you pinched Peter and called him names. You pushed him off the comfy black chair. You screamed. You wouldn't eat your sprouts. You—'

'Aside from *that*,' said Horrid Henry. 'I've been *so* good. I deserve a grump card.'

'Henry,' said Dad. 'You know we only give grump cards for *exceptionally* good behaviour.'

'But I never get one!' howled Henry.

Mum and Dad looked at each other.

'And why do you think that is?' said Mum.

'Because you're mean and unfair and the worst parents in the world!' screamed Horrid Henry.

What other reason could there be?

A grump card was precious beyond gold and silver and rubies and diamonds. If Mum or Dad thought you'd behaved totally brilliantly above and beyond the call of duty they gave you a grump card. A grump card meant that you could erase any future punishment. A grump card was a glittering, golden, get-out-of-jail-free ticket.

Horrid Henry had never had a grump

card. Just think, if he had even one . . .
if Dad was in the middle of telling him
off, or banning him from the computer
for a week, all Henry had to do was
hand him a grump card, and, like
magic, the telling off would end, the
punishment would be erased, and Henry
would be back on the computer zapping
baddies.

Horrid Henry longed for a grump
card. But how could he ever get one?

Even Peter, who was always perfect, only had seven. And he'd never even used a single one. What a waste. What a total waste.

Imagine what he could do if he had a grump card . . . He could scoff every sweet and biscuit and treat in the house. He could forget all about homework and watch telly instead. And best of all, if Dad ever tried to ban him from the computer, or Mum shouted that he'd lost his pocket money for a month, all Henry had to do was produce the magic card.

What bliss.

What heaven.

What joy.

But *how* could Henry get a grump card? How? How?

Could he behave totally brilliantly above and beyond the call of duty?

Horrid Henry considered. Nah. That was impossible. He'd once spent a whole day being perfect, and even then had ended up being sent to his room.

So how else to get a grump card?

Steal one? Hmmm. Tempting. Very tempting. He could sneak into Peter's room, snatch a grump card or two, then sneak out again. He could even substitute a fake grump card at the bottom in case Peter noticed his stash

was smaller. But then Peter would
be sure to tell on him when Henry
produced the golden ticket to freedom,
and Mum and Dad would be so cross
they'd probably *double* his punishment
and ban him from the computer
for life.

Or, he could kidnap Fluff Puff, Peter's
favourite plastic sheep, and hold

 him for ransom. Yes!
And then when Peter
had ransomed him back,
Henry could steal him
again. And again. Until
all Peter's grump cards
were his. Yes! He was brilliant. He was
a genius. Why had he never thought of
this before?

Except . . . if Peter told on him,
Henry had a horrible feeling that he
would get into trouble. Big big trouble

that not even a grump card could get him out of.

Time to think again. Could he swap something for one? What did Henry have that Peter wanted? Comics? No. Crisps? No. Killer Boy Rats CDs? No way.

Henry sighed. Maybe he could *buy* one from Peter. Unfortunately, Horrid Henry never had any money. Whatever pitiful pocket money he ever had always seemed to vanish through his fingers. Besides, who'd want to give that wormy worm a penny?

Better yet, could Henry *trick* Peter into giving him one? Yeah! They could play a great game called *Learn to Share*. Henry could tell Peter to give him half his grump cards as Peter needed to learn to stop being such a selfish hog. It *could* work . . .

There was a snuffling sound, like a pig rustling for truffles, and Perfect Peter stuck his head round the door.

'What are you doing, Henry?' asked Peter.

'None of your business,

worm,' said Horrid Henry.

'Want to play with me?' said Peter.

'No,' said Henry. Peter was always nagging Henry to play with him. But when Henry *had* played Robot and Mad Professor with him, for some reason Peter hadn't enjoyed giving Henry all his sweets and money and doing all Henry's chores for him.

'We could play checkers . . . or Scrabble?' said Peter.

'N-O spells no,' said Henry. 'Now get out of—' Horrid Henry paused. Wait a minute. Wait a minute . . .

'How much will you pay me?' said Horrid Henry.

Perfect Peter stared at Henry.

'Pay you? *Pay* you to play with me?'

'Yeah,' said Henry.

Perfect Peter considered.

'How much?' said Peter slowly.

'One pound a minute,' said Henry.

'One pound a minute!' said Peter.

'It's a good offer, toad,' said Henry.

'No it isn't,' said Peter.

'What, you think it should be two pounds a minute?' said Henry. 'Okay.'

'I'm going to tell on you,' said Peter.

'Tell what, worm? That I made you a perfectly good offer? No one's forcing you.'

Perfect Peter paused. Henry was right. He could just say no.

'Or . . .' said Horrid Henry. 'You could pay me in grump cards.'

'Grump cards?' said Peter.

'After all, you have tons and you never use them,' said Henry. 'You could spare one or two or four and never notice . . . and you'll refill your stash in no time.'

It was true that he didn't really need his grump cards, thought Peter. And it would be so nice to play a game . . .

'Okay,' said Peter.

YES! thought Horrid Henry. What a genius he was.

'I charge one grump card a minute.'

'No,' said Peter. 'Grump cards are valuable.'

Horrid Henry sighed.

'Tell you what, because I'm such a nice brother, I will play you a game of Scra . . . Scrab . . .' Horrid Henry could barely bring himself to even say the word *Scrabble* . . . 'for two grump cards. And a game of checkers for two more.'

'And a soft toy tea party?' said Peter.
Did anyone suffer as much as Henry?
He sighed, loudly.

'Okay,' said Horrid Henry. 'But that'll
cost you three.'

Horrid Henry stared happily at his seven
glorious grump cards. He'd done it! He
was free to do anything he wanted. He
would be king for ever.

Why wait?

Horrid Henry skipped downstairs, went straight to the sweet jar, and took a huge handful of sweets.

'Put those back, Henry,' said Mum. 'You know sweet day is Saturday.'

'Don't care,' said Henry. 'I want sweets now and I'm having them now.' Shoving the huge handful into his mouth, he reached into the jar for more.

'Henry!' screamed Mum. 'Put those back. That's it. No sweets for a week. Now go straight—'

Horrid Henry whipped out a grump card and handed it to Mum.

Mum gasped. Her jaw dropped.

'Where . . . when . . . did you get a grump card?'

Henry shrugged. 'I got it 'cause I was so good.'

Mum stared at him. Dad must have given him one. How amazing.

Henry strolled into the sitting room. Time for *Terminator Gladiator*!

Dad was sitting on the sofa watching the boring news. Well, not for long. Horrid Henry grabbed the clicker and switched channels.

'Hey,' said Dad. 'I was watching.'

'Tough,' said Henry. 'I'm watching what I want to watch. Go Gladiator!' he squealed.

'Don't be horrid, Henry. I'm warning you . . .'

Horrid Henry stuck out his tongue at Dad. 'Buzz off, baldie.'

Dad gasped.

'That's it, Henry. No computer games for a week. Now go straight—'

Dad stared at the grump card which Henry waved at him. Henry? A grump card? Mum must have given him one. But how? When?

'I'll just go off now and play on the computer,' said Henry, smirking.

Tee hee. The look on Dad's face. And what fun to play on the computer, after he'd been banned from it! That was well worth a grump card. After all, he had plenty.

Horrid Henry spat his sprouts onto the floor. But a grump card took care of the 'no TV for the rest of the day' punishment. Then he flicked peas at Peter and nicked four of his chips. That was well worth a grump card, too, thought Horrid Henry, to get his pocket money back. Bit of a shame that he had to give two grump cards to lift the ban on going to Ralph's sleepover, but, hey, that's what grump cards were for, right?

'Henry, it's my turn to play on the computer,' said Peter.

'Tough,' said Horrid Henry, zapping and blasting.

'I'm going to tell on you,' said Peter.

'Go ahead,' said Henry. 'See if I care.'

'You're going to get into big, big trouble,' said Peter.

'Go away, wormy worm toady pants poopsicle,' said Henry. 'You're annoying me.'

'Mum! Henry just called me a wormy worm toady pants poopsicle!' shrieked Peter.

'Henry! Stop calling your brother names,' said Mum.

'I didn't,' shouted Henry.

'He did too!' howled Peter.

'Shut up, Ugg-face!' snarled Henry.

'Mum! Henry just called me Ugg-face!'

'That's it,' said Mum. 'Henry! Go to your room. No computer for a—'

Horrid Henry handed over another grump card.

'Henry. Where did you get these?' said Mum.

'I was given them for being good,' said Horrid Henry. That wasn't a lie, because he *had* been good by playing with Peter, and Peter had given them to him.

Perfect Peter burst into tears.

'Henry tricked me,' said Peter. 'He took my grump cards.'

'Didn't.'

'Did.'

'We made a deal, you wibble-face
nappy!' shrieked Henry, and attacked.
He was a bulldozer flattening a wriggling
worm . . .

'AAARRRGGGHH!' screamed Peter.

'You horrid boy,' said Mum. 'No
pocket money for a week. No TV for
a week. No computer for a week. No
sweets for a week. Go to your room!'

Whoa, grump card to the rescue.
Thank goodness he'd saved one for
emergencies.

What? Huh?

Horrid Henry felt frantically inside his pockets. He looked on the floor. He checked his pockets again. And again.

There were no grump cards left.

What had he done? Had he just blown all his grump cards in an hour? His precious, precious grump cards?

The grump cards he'd never, ever get again?

NOOOOOOOOO!!!!!!!

4

HORRID HENRY'S OLYMPICS

Chomp chomp chomp chomp . . .
Burp.

Ahhh! Horrid Henry scoffed the last crumb of Super Spicy Hedgehog crisps and burped again. So yummy. Wow. He'd eaten the entire pack in seventeen seconds. No one could guzzle crisps faster than Horrid Henry, especially when he was having to gobble them secretly in class. He'd never been caught, not even—

A dark, icy shadow fell across him.

'Are you eating in class, Henry?' hissed Miss Battle-Axe.

'No,' said Henry.

Tee hee. Thanks to his super-speedy jaws, he'd *already* swallowed the evidence.

'Then where did this crisp packet come from?' said Miss Battle-Axe, pointing to the plastic bag on the floor.

Henry shrugged.

'Bert! Is this yours?'

'I dunno,' said Beefy Bert.

'There is *no* eating in class,' said Miss Battle-Axe. Why did she have to say the same things over and over? One day the Queen would discover that she, Boudicca Battle-Axe, was her long-lost daughter and sweep her off to the palace, where she would live a life of pampered luxury. But until then—

'Now, as I was saying, before I was so rudely interrupted,' she glared at Horrid

Henry, 'our school will be having its
very own Olympics. We'll be running
and jumping and swimming and—'

'Eating!' yelled Horrid Henry.

'Quiet, Henry,' snapped Miss Battle-
Axe. 'I want all of you to practise hard,
both in school and out, to show—'

Horrid Henry stopped listening. It
was so unfair. Wasn't it bad enough that
every morning he had to heave his heavy
bones out of bed to go to school, without

75

wasting any of his precious TV-watching time running and jumping and swimming? He was a terrible runner. He was a pathetic jumper. He was a hopeless swimmer – though he did have his five-metre badge . . . Besides, Aerobic Al was sure to win every medal. In fact they should just give them all to him now and save everyone else a load of bother.

Shame, thought Horrid Henry, that the things he was so good at never got prizes. If there was a medal for who could watch TV the longest, or who could eat the most sweets, or who was quickest out of the classroom door when the home bell rang, well, he'd be covered in gold from head to toe.

'Go on, Susan! Jump higher.'

'I'm jumping as high as I can,' said Sour Susan.

'That's not high,' said Moody
Margaret. 'A tortoise could jump higher
than you.'

'Then get a tortoise,' snapped Susan
sourly.

'You're just a lazy lump.'
'You're just a moody meanie.'
'Lump.'
'Meanie.'
'LUMP!'

'MEANIE!'

Slap!

Slap!

'Whatcha doin'?' asked Horrid Henry, leaning over the garden wall.

'Go away, Henry,' said Margaret.

'Yeah, Henry,' said Susan.

'I can stand in my own garden if I want to,' said Henry.

'Just ignore him,' said Margaret.

'We're practising for the school Olympics,' said Susan.

Horrid Henry snorted.

'I don't see *you* practising,' said Margaret.

'That's 'cause I'm doing my *own* Olympics, frog-face,' said Henry.

His jaw dropped. YES! YES! A thousand times yes! Why hadn't he thought of this before? Of course he should set up his own Olympics.

And have the competitions he'd always wanted to have. A name-calling competition! A chocolate-eating competition! A crisp-eating competition! A who-could-watch-the-most-TVs-at-the-same-time-competition! He'd make sure he had competitions that *he* could win. The Henry Olympics. The Holympics. And the prizes would be . . . the prizes would be . . . masses and masses of chocolate!

'Can Ted and Gordon

79

and I be in your
Olympics?' said
Perfect Peter.

'NO!' said
Henry. Who'd
want some nappy
babies competing?
They'd spoil everything, they'd—

Wait a minute . . .

'Of course you can, Peter,' said Henry
smoothly. 'That will be one pound
each.'

'Why?' said Ted.

'To pay for the super fantastic
prizes, of course,' said Henry. 'Each
champion will win a massive prize of . . .
chocolate!'

Peter's face fell.

'Oh,' he said.

'And a medal,' added Henry quickly.

'Oh,' said Peter, beaming.

'How massive?' said Margaret.

'Armfuls and armfuls,' said Horrid Henry. His mouth watered just thinking about it.

'Hmmm,' said Margaret. 'Well, I think there should be a speed haircutting competition. And dancing.'

'Dancing?' said Henry. Well, why not? He was a brilliant dancer. His elephant stomp would win any competition

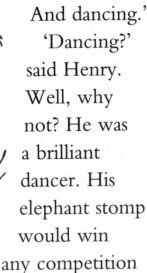

hands down. 'Okay.'

Margaret and Susan plonked down one pound each.

'By the way, that's *ballroom* dancing,' said Margaret.

'No way,' said Henry.

'No ballroom dancing, then we won't enter,' said Margaret. 'And Linda and Gurinder and Kate and Fiona and Soraya won't either.'

Horrid Henry considered. He was sure to win everything else, so why not let her have a tiny victory? And the more people who entered, the more chocolate for him!

'Okay,' said Henry.

'Bet you're scared I'll win everything,' said Margaret.

'Am not.'

'Are too.'

'I can eat more sweets than you any day.'

'Ha!' said Margaret. 'I'd like to see you try.'

'The Purple Hand Gang can beat the Secret Club *and* the Best Boys Club, no sweat,' said Horrid Henry. 'Bring it on.'

★

THE REAL OLYMPICS ARE HERE!

TIRED OF BORING OLD SWIMMING AND RUNNING? OF COURSE YOU ARE!

NOW'S YOUR CHANCE TO COMPETE IN THE

HOLYMPICS

THE GREATEST OLYMPICS OF ALL!!!

SPEED-EATING SWEETS! TV WATCHING! CRISP EATING! BURP TO THE BEAT!

BALLROOM DANCING. SPEED HAIRCUTTING.

Entry Fee £1 for the chance to win loads of chocolate!!!!!

'Hang on,' said Margaret. 'What's with calling this the Holympics? It should be the Molympics. I came up with the haircutting and dancing competitions.'

''Cause Molympics is a terrible name,' said Henry.

'So's Holympics,' said Margaret.

'Actually,' said Peter, 'I think it should be called the Polympics.'

'Shut up, worm,' said Henry.

'Yeah, worm,' said Margaret.

'Mum!' screamed Henry. '**MUM!!!!!!!!**'

Mum came running out of the shower.

'What is it, Henry?' she said, dripping water all over the floor. 'Are you all right?'

'I need sweets,' he said.

'You got me out of the shower because you need sweets?' she repeated.

'I need to practise for the sweet speed-
eating competition,' said Henry. 'For my
Olympics.'

'Absolutely not,' said Mum.

Horrid Henry was outraged.

'How am I supposed to win if I can't
practise?' he howled. 'You're always
telling me to practise stuff. And now
when I want to you won't let me.'

Bookings for Henry's Olympics were
brisk. Everyone in Henry's class – and a

few from Peter's – wanted to compete.
Horrid Henry gazed happily at the £45
pounds' worth of chocolate and crisps
piled high on his bed. Wow. Wow.
Mega mega wow. Boxes and boxes
and boxes filled with yummy, yummy
sweets! Giant bar after giant bar of
chocolate. His Holympics would have
the best prizes ever. And he, Henry,
fully expected to win most of them.
He'd win enough chocolate to last him a
lifetime AND have the glory of coming
first, for once.

Horrid Henry gazed at the chocolate
prize mountain.

The chocolate prize mountain gazed
back at him, and winked.

Wait.

He, Henry, was doing ALL the work.
Surely it was only fair if he got *something*
for his valuable time. He should have

kept a bit of money
back to cover his
expenses.

Horrid Henry
removed a giant
chocolate bar from
the pile.

After all, I do need
to practise for the
speed-eating contest,
he thought, tearing
off the wrapper and

shoving a massive piece into his mouth.
And then another. Oh boy, was that
chocolate yummy. In a few seconds, it
was gone.

Yeah! Horrid Henry, chocolate-eating
champion of the universe!

You know, thought Henry, gazing
at the chocolate mound teetering
precariously on his bed, I think I bought
too many prizes. And I *do* need to
practise for my event . . .

What a great day, thought Horrid Henry
happily. He'd won the sweet speed-
eating competition (though Greedy
Graham had come a close second), the
crisp-eating contest AND the name-
calling one. (Peter had run off screaming
when Henry called him Wibble Wobble
Pants, Nappy Noodle, and Odiferous.)

Rude Ralph won 'Burp to the

Beat'. Margaret and Susan won best
ballroom dancers. Vain Violet was the
surprise winner of the speed haircutting
competition. Weepy William
. . . well, his hair would grow back –
eventually.

Best of all, Aerobic Al didn't win a
thing.

The winners gathered round to collect
their prizes.

'Where's my chocolate, Henry?' said Moody Margaret.

'And there had better be loads like you promised,' said Vain Violet.

Horrid Henry reached into the big prize bag.

Now, where was the ballroom dancing prize?

He pulled out a Choco Bloco. Yikes, was that all the chocolate he had left? He rummaged around some more.

'A Choco Bloco?' said Margaret slowly. 'A *single* Choco Bloco?'

'They're very yummy,' said Henry.

'And mine?' said Violet.

'And mine?' said Ralph.

'And mine for coming second?' said Graham.

'You're meant to share it!' screamed Horrid Henry, as he turned and ran.

Wow, thought Horrid Henry, as
he fled down the road, Rude Ralph,
Moody Margaret, Sour Susan, Vain
Violet, and Greedy Graham chasing
after him, I'm pretty fast when I need
to be. Maybe I *should* enter the school
Olympics after all.

Acknowledgments

Thanks to Imogen Stubbs
for sharing some fine film-making
moments with me.

HORRiD HENRY BOOKS

Colour books

Early Readers

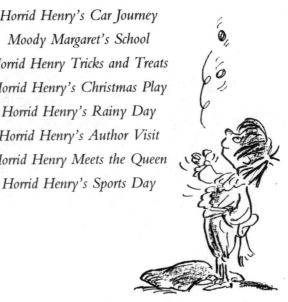

Horrid Henry is also available on CD and as a digital download, all read by Miranda Richardson.

"A hoot from beginning to end . . .
As always, Miranda Richardson's delivery is perfection and the manic music is a delight."
Daily Express

'Long may this dreadful boy continue to terrorise all who know him. He's a nightmare, but so entertaining . . . Miranda Richardson's spirited reading is accompanied by a brilliant music soundtrack – they make a noisy and fun-filled duo.'
Parents' Guide

HORRiD HENRY

The first book about the adventures of Horrid Henry, in which Henry tries (unbelievably) to be good, goes to dance classes, makes 'Glop' with Moody Margaret and goes on holiday.

'Henry is a truly great character'
Sunday Times

HORRiD HENRY
Gets Rich Quick

Horrid Henry makes sure he gets the presents
he wants for Christmas, sabotages the school
sports day, runs away from home, and thinks
of a brilliant way to get rich quick.

HORRID HENRY
Robs the Bank

Horrid Henry helps himself to all the money
he needs to win his favourite board game,
comes up with another spectacular money-
making scheme for launching a newspaper
with all the school gossip, vows vengeance on
Perfect Peter when Peter steals his birthday
party theme and has his own Pirate Party, then
takes over as Head Teacher when Peter plays
school with his goody-goody friends.

HORRiD HENRY
Wakes the Dead

Horrid Henry
finds a sure-fire way of
wielding the remote control
to ensure he always watches his
programme of choice, vies with
Moody Margaret to become the head
of the school, shows off his prowess as
a magician in the school talent show, and
battles it out with Perfect Peter over who
gets the green dinosaur and who gets the
purple one.

HORRiD HENRY
Rocks

Horrid Henry and Perfect Peter keep
invading each other's rooms, Moody Margaret
invites the Secret Club for a sleepover, with
catastrophic results, Miss Battle-Axe's class have
to write their autobiographies, the best to be
published in the local paper, and Horrid Henry
wants to go to the Killer Boy Rats concert not
the Daffy and her Dancing Daisies concert –
what can Henry do?

HORRID HENRY
and the Zombie Vampire

Horrid Henry terrorizes his classmates at a
school sleepover in the museum, plays with
Perfect Peter and tricks him into handing over
all his money, gets out of writing his own story
for Miss Battle-Axe by adapting one of Peter's,
and meets the Nudie Foodie, a celebrity chef,
who comes to the school to improve
school dinners. No more burgers!
No more chips!